Crawley
the Lobster

Written by Carola Livingston

Illustrations by Crary Brouhard

Text copyright © 2016 by Carola C. Livingston and Illustrations by Crary Brouhard copyright © 2016
Edited by Winona Mullis, Graphic Design by Crary Brouhard

A Lobster family lived way out in the ocean. Crawley Lobster had a brother named Whitey, who was named so because of the white spots on his shell. Most of the family had reddish shells without white spots.

Crawley loved to explore all day long and was allowed to wander off trying out his legs. His parents would remind him to stay within the boundaries of the lobster village and not to go beyond the big rock at the edge, marking the open waters.

Since his brother Whitey was more noticable due to his unique white spots, his parents kept a closer eye on him and asked him to stay closer to home. But Whitey would often watch his brother explore and he was always excited to listen to Crawley's stories when he came home.

One day Crawley happened to crawl farther than usual. The water was getting very rough on the surface of the ocean and Crawley could hear pounding on a nearby beach. He turned to go home, but realized he had made many turns and lost his way!

"Oh, no," he thought, "I should have listened to my parents and paid attention."

Tossed
and
turned
around,

        not sure what he should do next,
        Crawley noticed a cave nearby

              and
              headed
              in that
              direction.

When he reached the cave, the waves sounded as if they were crashing above his head. Scared, he decided to crawl in and rest. Exhausted from his journey, of course, he fell asleep.

When he awoke, Crawley saw there was very little water in the cave. Looking out of his cave, he saw the water had disappeared from the beach.

He watched with fascination as waves formed a dark peak and then started to fall in bubbles that almost looked like crystals.

It was beautiful for Crawley to listen to the pounding roar, while watching the waves tumble upon each other then run back down the beach to the ocean to join the other waves coming in.

The shore seemed to dance with beads of foam pearls.

Crawley realized that he had never known what the pounding noise above him had been. He had never seen a wave before!

As time went by, he lay in a puddle in the cave to keep him wet. He began to realize his parents would worry when he did not come home. Crawley knew he was in trouble. The waves were too strong for him to walk into and the water had moved way down the beach so that only sand was near his cave.

Then he heard a familiar sound! He looked out the cave and almost didn't believe his eyes! He saw what he thought was his brother Whitey's head pop out of a big wave! It quickly disappeared back under the water. Crawley wondered if he really saw his brother or if he had been dreaming. He wished he could see him again.

Sometime later he saw his father's head pop out of the wave. He knew this time he was not dreaming! His brother had brought Crawley help, but the waves were even too strong for his father to ride through. Crawley's father tried and tried to get closer to the cave but kept getting knocked down by the waves into the ocean.

Every so often, Crawley's father's or brother's head would appear at the surface only to disappear again.

After what seemed like days to Crawley, but was really hours, the water started to creep up toward the cave. Finally it reached the place where Crawley could re-enter the water, so he did just that.

Of course, his father and brother were there to greet him. Everyone was so glad he was back in the water. They clapped their front two claws together to show they were happy and Crawley responded the same way. He wanted to thank his brother for getting help and finding him.

They headed back toward home with Crawley's father leading the way. As they swam, the father pointed to a funny looking cage and shook his claws. He told Crawley and Whitey they were never to go near those cages because they were dangerous for lobsters.

As they continued swimming home they saw a cage with a squealing lobster in it being pulled up by ropes to the surface. They knew the lobster would probably never return. After Crawley's recent experience, he knew he would listen better to his parents advice from now on. They knew the hazards in the world and what to do to stay out of trouble.

If you ever swim under the water near where they live, Crawley and Whitey might be seen happily playing near their ocean home.